Jorgensen

CAN YOU SOLVE THE MYSTERY?

READ THE
SOLUTIONS
IN YOUR
MIRROR

Hawkeye Collins & Amy Adams in

THE CASE OF THE FAMOUS
Chocolate
Chip Cookies
& 8 OTHER MYSTERIES

by M. MASTERS

This book is dedicated to all the children across
the country who helped us develop the *Can You
Solve the Mystery?*™ series.

Reprinted by Abdo & Daughters 1994

Library of Congress Cataloging in Publication Data

Masters, M.
Hawkeye Collins and Amy Adams in The case of the
famous chocolate chip cookies & 8 other mysteries.

  (Can you solve the mystery? ; #6)
  Summary: Hawkeye Collins and Amy Adams, two
twelve-year-old sleuths, solve nine mysteries using
Hawkeye's sketches of important clues. The reader
is asked to use Hawkeye's sketches and hints to
solve the mysteries.
  [1. Mystery and detective stories. 2. Literary
recreations.] I. Title. II. Title: Hawkeye Collins
and Amy Adams in The case of the famous chocolate
chip cookies & 8 other mysteries. III. Title: Case of the
famous chocolate chip cookies & 8 other mysteries.
IV. Series: Masters, M. Can you solve the
mystery? ; #6.
PZ7.M42392HAWM   1983   [Fic]   83-11439

Printed in the United States of America

Copyright© 1983 by Meadowbrook Creations.

All stories written by Lani and David Havens.
Illustrations by Stephen Cardot and Brett Gadbois.

Editor: Kathe Grooms
Assistant Editor: Louise Delagran
Consulting Editor: R.D. Zimmerman
Design: Terry Dugan
Production: John Ware, Donna Ahrens, Pamela Barnard
Cover Art: Robert Sauber

CONTENTS

READ THE SOLUTIONS IN YOUR MIRROR

Amy Adams

Hawkeye Collins

Young Sleuths Detect Fun in Mysteries

By Alice Cory
Staff Writer

Lakewood Hills has two new super sleuths watching over its citizens. They are Christopher "Hawkeye" Collins and Amy Amanda Adams, both 12 years old and sixth-grade students at Lakewood Hills Elementary.

Christopher Collins, the popular, blond, blue-eyed sleuth of 128 Crestview Drive, is better known by his nickname, "Hawkeye." His father, Peter Collins, who is an attorney downtown, explains, "We started calling him Hawkeye many years ago because he notices everything, even tiny details. That's what makes him so good at solving mysteries." His mother, Linda Collins, a real estate agent, agrees: "Yes, but he

Sleuths continued on page 4A

Sleuths continued from page 2A

also started to draw at a very early age. His sketches capture everything he sees. He draws clues or the scene of the crime — or anything else that will help solve a mystery."

Amy Adams, a spitfire with red hair and sparkling green eyes, lives right across the street, at 131 Crestview Drive. Known to many as the star of the track team, she is also a star math student. "She's quick of mind, quick of foot and quick of temper," says her teacher, Ted Bronson, chuckling. "And she's never intimidated." Not only do she and Hawkeye share the same birthday, but also the same love of mysteries.

"If something's wrong," says Amy, leaning on her ten-speed, "you just can't look the other way."

"Right," says Hawkeye, pulling his ever-present sketch pad and pencil from his back pocket. "And if we can't solve a case right away, I'll do a drawing of the scene of the crime. When we study my sketch, we can usually figure out what happened."

When the two detectives are not playing video games or soccer (Hawkeye is the captain of the sixth-grade team), they can often be seen biking around town, making sure justice is done. Occa-sionally aided by Hawkeye's frisky golden retriever, Nosey, and Amy's six-year-old sister, Lucy, they've solved every case they've handled to date.

How did the two get started in the detective business?

It all started last year at Lakewood Hills Elementary's Career Days. There the two met Sergeant Treadwell, one of Lakewood Hills' best-known policemen. Of Hawkeye and Amy, Sergeant Treadwell proudly brags, "They're terrific. Right after we met, one of the teachers had a whole pile of tests stolen. I sure couldn't figure out who had done it, but Hawkeye did one of his sketches and he and Amy had the case solved in five minutes! You can't fool those two."

Sergeant Treadwell adds: "I don't know what Lakewood Hills ever did without Hawkeye and Amy. They've found a dognapped dog, located stolen video games, and cracked many other tough cases. Why, whenever I have a problem I can't solve, I know just where to go — straight to those two super sleuths!"

> **" They've found a dognapped dog, located stolen video games, and cracked many other tough cases. "**

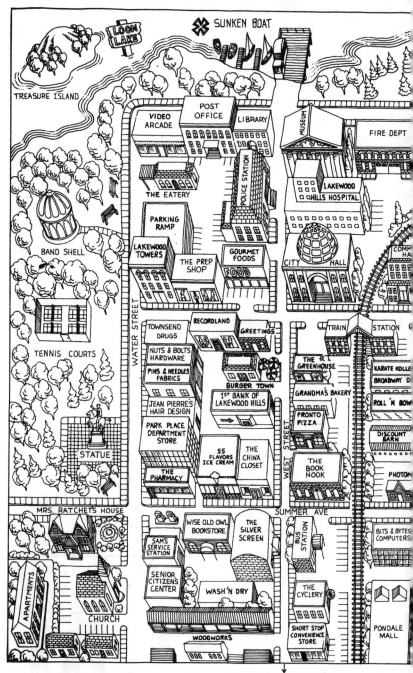

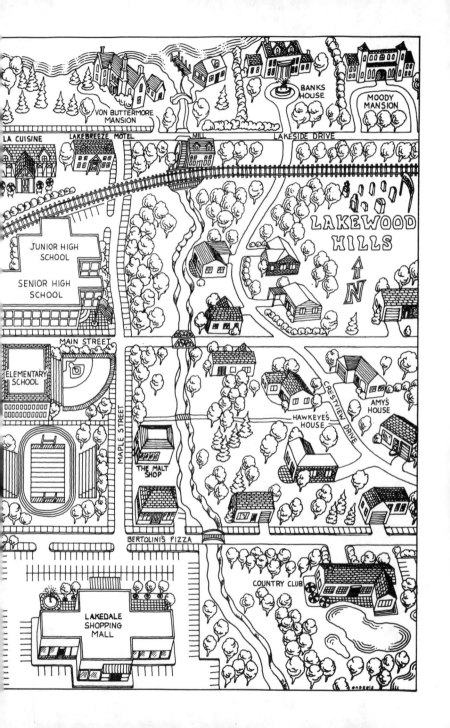

Dear Readers,

You can solve these mysteries along with us! Start by reading very carefully -- Watch out for things like what people <u>say</u> happened, the ways they behave, and details like the time and the weather.

Then look closely at the sketch or other picture clue with the story. If you remember the facts, the picture clue should help you break the case.

If you want to check your answer-- or if a hard case stumps you -- turn to the solutions at the back of the book. They're written in mirror type. Hold them up to a mirror and they'll look right. If you don't have a mirror, turn the page and hold it up to the light. (You can teach yourself to read backwards, too. We can do it pretty well now and it comes in handy some times in our cases.)

Have fun -- we sure did!

Amy

Hawkeye

The Case of the Grand Canyon Rescue

Deep within the Grand Canyon, Hawkeye Collins and Amy Adams slid off their burros. Amy's parents, her sister Lucy, and their park-ranger guide were just up ahead.

The Adams family had invited Amy's good friend, Hawkeye, to vacation with them while his parents were in Europe on business. Hawkeye and Amy lived across the street from each other in Lakewood Hills, Minnesota. The two friends loved nothing better than solving mysteries—but this trip was turning out to be almost as much fun as an unsolved case.

"Man, the Grand Canyon really is an awesome place," said Hawkeye. "It's like the moon or something. My parents'll never believe we camped here—I wish they could have come."

"Me, too." Amy brushed her red hair out of her eyes and glanced up the steep trail they had just come down. "For thrills a minute, that trail was better than a spook house."

They were helping the park ranger and Amy's parents unload their packs when they heard a roar come over the edge of the steep canyon walls.

"A helicopter!" shouted Lucy, pointing to the sky.

"Everybody grab your reins!" shouted the park ranger.

They all dashed over to their burros and held them by the reins. The animals snorted and reared in fear as the chopper came closer and closer. Finally the helicopter landed and another park ranger sprang out of the cockpit.

"John!" he yelled to the ranger who was guiding Amy's family. "There's a kid missing. Probably east of Elephant Rock. She's been gone since last night. Can you search the east trail area?"

John turned to Mr. and Mrs. Adams. "Do you folks think you can go ahead and set up camp? If we do locate the girl, this will be the closest base camp."

Mr. Adams nodded. "Of course."

John pulled a map out of his hip pocket. "Here's where I'll be going. Elephant Rock is a mile-long rock formation. It's kind of like an island, only there's no water around it. There are two trails that split and run to the east and west. They go around the rock and join together again at the northern tip."

Mrs. Adams glanced at her watch. "Not much daylight left, John."

"Yeah, I'd better get going. That east trail is terrible." John handed a walkie-talkie to them. "Here, keep this in case I need to relay any messages to you. I'll have the second one with me, right here in my saddle bag."

John talked to the other ranger briefly. Then he jumped on his burro and trotted off. The helicopter took off in a cloud of dust.

"Man, I sure hope he find*th* that little girl," said Lucy to her mother. "I think I'll *th*ee if I can help."

Lucy went over to a pack and struggled to get out a pair of binoculars. She then headed toward a low ridge.

"Don't go too far," called Mr. Adams.

"I won't," replied Lucy.

"You know," Hawkeye said to Amy, "the toothless wonder isn't all that bad. She's kind of a little spitfire—sort of like you, you know? She might even make a good sleuth someday."

Amy's sharp mind and lightning-fast thinking made her an excellent sleuth. She

3

was able to crack codes, see patterns, and figure things out with a speed that amazed most adults.

Lucy headed off in the brush while Hawkeye and Amy helped her parents set up the camp. When they were done, Hawkeye turned to Amy.

"Let's see what Lucy's turned up," he said.

"Sure thing," said Amy.

They spotted Lucy's blond head turning and turning, some distance away. She was sitting on top of a huge boulder, peering through her binoculars. Hawkeye and Amy hiked over to her.

"Any luck?" asked Amy, concern showing in her green eyes.

"Naw." Lucy handed the binoculars to Hawkeye. "Here, Hawkeye, you're the one with the sharp eye*th*. *Th*ee what you can find."

"Hope I see something," he said, a little doubtfully.

Hawkeye had gotten his nickname because of his ability to see things that other people never noticed. That power, paired with his terrific sketching skill, gave him a big advantage when he was trying to crack a case.

Concentrating hard, he slowly swept the canyon with the binoculars. Suddenly something moved into his field of vision. He pulled the binoculars away.

"Hey, look!" he cried, handing Amy the binoculars.

A lone burro, about half a mile away, was almost perfectly camouflaged by a large rock. It was all saddled and outfitted.

"But there's no rider!" said Amy.

"Come on!" said Lucy, sliding off the boulder and charging forward.

Amy burst into a run and, scrambling over the rocks, was the first to reach the riderless burro.

"There's a note attached to the stirrups!" she yelled back as Hawkeye and Lucy caught up with her.

"It's torn. But I bet it's from the lost girl," she said, handing the note to Hawkeye.

"Let me *th*ee it, too," Lucy cried. "You guy*th*, it wa*th* my idea to look for the girl, you know. And I can read now."

"Okay, okay, Lucy. Fair enough." Amy handed it to her. "What do you make of it?"

Lucy snatched it and read it slowly, word by word, her lips moving silently. She shrugged and handed the note back to Amy.

"Well, at lea*th*t the little girl'*th* out of the *th*un," said Lucy.

"Hey, wait a minute," said Amy, studying the note. "That explains the last line."

HELP!
I Hurt my leg this mor
when I Fell off my Bur
And I can't mov
Please hurry becaus
very thirsty even th
I'm in the Shad
I'm on the w
side of Elep
Jes

Lucy snatched the note and read it slowly, word by word, her lips moving silently.

"That means—" began Hawkeye.

"Right," said Amy, starting back toward her parents. "That means we know where the girl is."

WHERE WAS THE MISSING GIRL?

See page 77

The Mystery of the Lily Switcher

It was Saturday morning. Hawkeye rolled out of bed, pulled on his jeans and his grey sweat shirt, ran his fingers through his blond hair, and quietly tiptoed out to the kitchen.

As usual, Nosey, Hawkeye's golden retriever, was already there. She was waiting for him right in front of the refrigerator. Nosey wagged her tail, lifted one paw and then the other, and barked.

"Aw, Nosey," groaned Hawkeye. "Give me a break!"

But Nosey, determined to get a handout of any sort, went through her full routine of tricks. She lay down, rolled over, and played dead. Sensing that this was still not enough, Nosey then ran over to the phone. As she tried to do her new trick—answering the phone—she struggled to grab the receiver with her mouth.

"No!" Hawkeye said in a hoarse whisper, as he lunged for the phone. "You're not supposed to do that trick anymore. You've already hung up on six people!"

He took the phone from Nosey and returned it to its cradle.

"Nosey, when it comes to food," Hawkeye snorted, "you've got about as much dignity as a worm."

But Nosey knew she had won, and she sat down in front of one of the cabinets, her tail beating from side to side. Hawkeye went to the cupboard and got out the box of dog biscuits.

"How come you always win?" he grumbled. "I mean—"

His words were cut off by loud, quick knocks on the back door.

"Hawkeye, it's me, Amy." There was a ring of urgency to his friend's voice. "Let me in. Hurry!"

Hawkeye tossed Nosey a biscuit, which she caught in mid-air, and then hustled over to the door. Amy started talking even before he had the door open.

"Come on," she said, motioning him outside. "Mr. Spinati just called from his greenhouse. Someone stole his prize lilies—the ones he was going to enter in a big flower show today!"

Hawkeye spun around. "I'll get my sketch pad!"

He grabbed his pad and pencil and put on his jean jacket. He was halfway to the door when he remembered something.

"Oops. Amy, wait a minute. I better leave Mom and Dad a note. They're still asleep."

Seconds later, the two sleuths were racing down Crestview Drive on their ten-speeds, with Nosey bounding after them.

"Mr. Spinati is really upset," said Amy as they turned onto Main Street. "I mean, he's kind of strange anyway, but I hope he hasn't flipped out totally."

Hawkeye laughed. "Remember when he told Mrs. Ratchet she was sour enough to wilt a crab apple tree?" He turned around and whistled to his dog. "Come on, Nosey, quit sniffing that tree!"

"Well, he's always been nice to my family," replied Amy. "Ever since Mom gave him a clipping from her begonia plant, he's sent her flowers every Mother's Day."

Imitating Mr. Spinati's deep voice, Amy said, "'To the mother of my begonias.'"

Laughing, she added, "That's what the note always says."

"Yeah, he can be pretty weird, but everybody says that he *does* grow the best flowers in the state," Hawkeye commented.

They rounded a corner and came to The Greenhouse. They propped their bikes against a tree and headed in, leaving Nosey outside.

Wringing his hands and muttering to himself, Mr. Spinati greeted them at the door. With quick, angry steps, he led them into the warm, humid greenhouse. The frosted windows softened the sunlight, but it was still very bright.

"Look at this!" he said, holding up a flowerpot full of wilted flowers. "My beautiful prize lilies—gone! Whoever snuck in and took them last night left these mangy-looking lilies in their place. Can you believe it? They thought I'd be fooled! They thought I wouldn't recognize my own babies!"

"You mean, someone broke in, took your lilies, and left these in their place?" asked Amy.

"Evidently so," Mr. Spinati said, looking around. "These are definitely not my flowers. But I don't know how the thief did it. The door was locked when I got here this morning, and I have the only key."

"Did you notice any broken windows or anything else?" asked Hawkeye, pulling out his sketch pad.

"No, nothing," snapped Mr. Spinati. "I checked everywhere, but—nothing!"

"Well," began Amy, trying another approach, "can you think of anyone who might have wanted to steal your plants?"

As they continued talking, Hawkeye began to draw. With quick, sure strokes, he outlined the scene and then began recording the details. Drawing sketches often helped Hawkeye to uncover clues.

"Oh, yes," said Mr. Spinati, putting his hand to his chin. "All sorts of people. Corbet, that rich florist from Baskerville Heights, would give his eyeteeth for my lilies. He keeps snooping around here asking questions, trying to figure out my secret for such huge blossoms. He's a big tall guy and he's always looking over my shoulder."

Mr. Spinati bent over, picked up the limp, pathetic plants, and continued.

"My lilies would have won first prize at the Lily Growers' Garden Show today. Anyone who was competing there would have wanted mine out of the way. After all, the prize was two thousand dollars."

Hawkeye whistled and looked up from the sketch. "Wow, that's a lot of money. How about anybody else? Any other suspects?"

Mr. Spinati scratched his balding head. "My old handyman, Gus Welker. He was a bitter little fellow—always in a snit because I wouldn't let him near my plants."

He picked up a handful of dirt, smelled it, then patted it back into place.

"I had to let him go—he made the plants so nervous! But he got a job the next day over at Davis Glass Company. Jack Davis, the owner, is probably having his own headaches about Gus by now." The old man stroked the leaves of a violet orchid.

Amy jumped into the conversation. "Hey, what about Mrs. Ratchet? You guys weren't—um, well, what would you say?— exactly friendly, were you?"

"No, never!" Mr. Spinati shook his head furiously. He glanced down at the wilted lilies. "Come to think of it, these poor things look like the kind of plants she'd grow!"

He sighed, put his hands to his face, and shook his head.

"But this isn't getting us any closer to my lilies. They're probably dying already!"

"Don't worry, we'll get them back," said Hawkeye, hurrying to finish his sketch. His blue eyes darted around the greenhouse.

Amy wandered over to the door and examined it. "That's right, we always—"

"Hey!" yelled Hawkeye suddenly. "I know how the thief got in!"

"Look at this!" said Mr. Spinati. "My beautiful prize lilies—gone!"

Amy rushed to his side and studied the drawing. Hawkeye silently pointed to something in it.

"You're right," she agreed. Then suddenly, she figured out something else.

"That's it!" she cried, her green eyes flashing in triumph. "I know who the thief was, too!"

WHO STOLE THE LILIES? HOW DID HE OR SHE DO IT?

See page 79

The Secret of the Carnival Cowboy

Late one Saturday afternoon, Hawkeye stood outside Amy's house and called, "Amy, come on! Sarge asked us to hurry! He's waiting at the Wild West Carnival grounds!"

Amy came stomping out of her house, wearing navy shorts and a yellow sleeveless top. "I'm trying to hurry, but Lucy, the toothless wonder, is trying to shake all the money out of her piggy bank."

It wasn't just that Amy's six-year-old sister, Lucy, wanted to help Hawkeye and Amy solve Sergeant Treadwell's new case. It was also that Lucy wanted to go to the Wild West Carnival herself. And she had pestered and pestered Hawkeye and Amy until they had finally agreed to take her along.

"Okay, okay," said Lucy as she bounded out of the house. "I'm all *thet*. Let'*th* go."

Hawkeye and Amy hopped on their ten-speeds and Lucy got on her banana bike, and the three of them took off. The carnival was set up in a large parking lot next to the old Lakewood Hills train station, on the edge of town.

They reached the lot a few minutes later. After locking their bikes to the bike rack, they hurried in, looking for Sergeant Treadwell.

"Sarge said to meet him at the photographer's stand near the corral," said Hawkeye, leading the way. The warm August breeze ruffled his blond hair.

Sergeant Treadwell was one of the six police officers in Lakewood Hills. He was a special friend of Hawkeye's and Amy's, and often asked for their help when a case proved difficult to crack. And many cases did, for although Sarge was a good cop, he was a poor detective.

"Over there!" said Lucy loudly, pointing through the crowd. "There he i*th*!"

Across the way, next to the photographer's stand and a caramel corn stand, stood Sergeant Treadwell. Leaning against a post right near him was a tall high-school kid.

"Hey, that's Lance Farley with him," said Amy. "I haven't seen him since he tried to steal my bike."

They cut through the swarms of people and made their way over to Sergeant Treadwell.

"Hi, Sarge," said Hawkeye.

"Hawkeye and Amy! At last you're here. And there's Lucy." The pudgy sergeant grinned and held out a bag of caramel corn in greeting. "Glad you guys could make it. Care for a little treat?"

Lucy jabbed her hand into the bag. "Thanks. What's the prob, *Th*arge?"

Sergeant Treadwell cleared his throat. "There was a fire behind Wilson's garage about noon today. A witness claims he saw Lance running away from the garage just before the fire broke out."

"That's a pack of lies," Lance broke in loudly. "I've been here all day. My picture proves it."

Sergeant Treadwell turned to Hawkeye and Amy and showed them a photograph. "Lance says this picture proves that he was here when the fire started."

"Look," Hawkeye said, pointing to Lance's arm in the photograph. "You can see his watch. It says twelve o'clock."

"Well, couldn't the picture have been taken in some other town or on some other day?" Amy asked. "This carnival's been to lots of other towns."

Lucy stood on her tip-toes and tried to see the picture. "Yeah, but you can *the*e the train *th*tation in the background. And today i*th* the fir*th*t day of the carnival."

"Well, I guess the picture must have been taken today," said Sergeant Treadwell, taking off his hat and scratching his head. "I hadn't thought about that."

Hawkeye stared at the photograph for a minute. "But—something's wrong," he muttered. Some detail in the picture was setting off an alarm in his mind, but he couldn't tell what it was yet.

Sergeant Treadwell looked stumped, too. He took another handful of caramel corn and munched on it thoughtfully.

Amy broke a long silence in the group. "Can I see the photo again?"

Sergeant Treadwell handed the photo to her. Lucy, trying to get another look, tugged on her sister's arm.

"Hey, look, Amy," said Lucy, pointing to the picture. "Look at that!"

"Holy cow, Lucy, you've done it!" Amy's green eyes twinkled. For the first time in many weeks, Amy gave her sister a big hug.

Hawkeye stared at the photograph for a minute. "But—something's wrong," he muttered.

"Hey, kid," she said. "You might be a sleuth yet! You've just proved that Lance *was* lying!"

WHAT DID LUCY SEE IN THE PHOTO?

See page 81

The Case of the Purse Snatcher's Snafu

Hawkeye and Amy came out of their karate class and squinted in the September sunshine. As they unlocked their ten-speeds, Amy pointed back to the building.

Amy said, "So Justin goes, 'I didn't mean to hurt you, Mr. Yamaguchi, honest, I—'"

"Help! Stop, thief! Stop that man! He stole my purse!"

Hawkeye and Amy looked up in time to see Mrs. Ratchet, the meanest person in Lakewood Hills, chasing a man toward them. He was in his twenties and wore faded jeans and a jean jacket.

With his sharp eyes, Hawkeye gauged the man's speed. At just the right moment, he stuck out his foot. The man tripped on it and went flying to the sidewalk.

"Let's get him!" Hawkeye shouted.

He and Amy jumped on the thief and tried to wrestle the purse away from him. Meanwhile, Mrs. Ratchet caught up with them and began swinging her shopping bag at the tangled mass of arms and legs.

"Hey, Mrs. Ratchet," yelled Amy. "Watch it! Don't hit us, we're trying to help!"

The thief suddenly pushed everyone away and scrambled to his feet. He broke into a run and dashed toward the Discount Barn. In a second, he had disappeared inside the front door.

"You beast!" screamed Mrs. Ratchet. "That's my purse!"

"We'll get him, Mrs. Ratchet," said Hawkeye. "You stay out here by the front door and make sure he doesn't come out this way."

Hawkeye and Amy jumped up and chased after the man, running as fast as they could into the store. It was jammed with shoppers.

Amy slapped her forehead. "Oh, brother. What a mess. It's the annual clearance sale. Practically everybody in Lakewood Hills is here. What a perfect way to give us the slip."

"Wait!" said Hawkeye. "I think I see him going down that aisle!"

The two of them tore down the main aisle, dodging shopping carts and baby strollers as they ran.

"Hey, you two!" shouted the store manager, Chuck McGuigan, chasing after them. "What are you doing?"

"Uh-oh," muttered Amy as she and Hawkeye stopped and waited for the manager to catch up. "I bet you he thinks we're shoplifting."

"Oh, it's you two," said Mr. McGuigan when he reached them. "Are you on a case or something?"

"A man stole Mrs. Ratchet's purse," explained Hawkeye. "We chased him in here."

Mr. McGuigan gasped. "That's terrible. Maybe he was trying to run through the store and get out the fire exit. It's the only other way out. Why don't you two go on and check the exit? I'll post a store detective at the front door and call the police."

"Sure thing," said Amy. "But where's the fire exit?"

"Go to the end of this aisle and turn left. It's three aisles over, behind the display with a couple of dummies dressed in sportswear." Mr. McGuigan hurried to the phone.

When they found the exit, Hawkeye said, "Man, I think we blew it this time. That guy could have doubled back and gone out the front door. Or he could still be somewhere inside the store. It's a million to one against our finding him."

Amy checked out the fire exit. "It's set to trigger an alarm if anyone opens it." She looked a little closer. "But it looks like someone played around with it. Why don't you do a quick sketch? We can show it to Mr. McGuigan and he can tell us if anything's wrong."

Hawkeye shrugged. "I guess there's nothing to lose."

He pulled his sketch pad and pencil out of his back pocket. Glancing at the scene around him, he quickly drew both the emergency exit and the rear of the store. In less than a minute, he had captured the entire scene.

When he was finished, Hawkeye studied the sketch for a moment, then shrugged and flipped his sketch pad shut. He stuffed it back into his pocket.

"Come on," said Amy. "Let's go find Mr. McGuigan."

They hadn't taken more than a few steps when Hawkeye froze. He pulled out his sketch pad again. He looked at it for a second, then gasped.

"Omigosh!" he muttered. He dropped his voice. *"The thief's ten feet away from us!*

"That guy could still be in the store. It's a million to one against our finding him," Hawkeye said.

Quick, Amy, run and get Mr. McGuigan—I'll stay right here and make sure the purse snatcher doesn't get away!"

WHERE WAS THE PURSE SNATCHER?

See page 83

The Mystery of the Treehouse Troublemaker

Amy couldn't believe the noise her friends could make.

"Order! Order!" shouted Mandy, hammering on the orange crate with a small block of wood.

But the angry voices continued at the Girls-Only Treehouse Club meeting. They had gathered in their beautiful new treehouse—with gold carpeting on the floor and yellow curtains on the windows—to try to figure out what to do about the break-in. Someone had stolen a bunch of things from their treasure box, and the five members were determined to do something about it.

"I just *know* it was the boys who took our stuff!" yelled Melissa. "You know how mad they are because we won't let any of 'em up here!"

"That's right," agreed Sara.

Kelly shouted, "Well, I say we should raid their hideout!"

"Will you guys shut up for one minute!" screamed Mandy at the top of her lungs. "Listen, I'm the president and if you guys don't quiet down, I'm—I'm gonna go!"

But the voices continued. Amy, the only non-member there, decided it was time for action. She put two fingers to her mouth and whistled as loudly as she could. Mandy, seated right next to her, covered her ears. Everyone else fell silent.

"Thanks, Amy," said Mandy, composing herself. "Now, one at a time."

"Madam President!" said Kelly, waving her hand.

"Yes," Mandy replied with grown-up politeness.

Kelly cleared her throat, hesitated, then spoke in a burst. "I think we should just go over there and rip the boys' hideout apart!"

Melissa leaped to her feet. "Yeah, and we should take everything we can grab!"

"Order! Order!" yelled Mandy, her voice growing hoarse. "Now, I brought Amy here to help us solve the case. Come on, you guys, please. Let's not do something stupid like raid the boys' hideout."

Just then someone called up from below. "Lizzy! Juliet has gotten out of her cage again! She's climbing up and down the curtains in the living room. Come on down and get her back into that cage in your bedroom. Right now, or else that raccoon will go back to the pet shop!"

Lizzy, the one quiet girl in the club, moaned. "Oh, no, not again. Boy, am I in for it." She stuck her head out the window. "Coming, Mom!"

With Mandy's help, Lizzy pulled open the trap door and swung down to the ladder.

"See you guys later," said Lizzy. "Let me know what we're going to do about this."

She scrambled down to the base of the large oak tree. Wasting no time, she ran to her back door, only twenty feet away.

When all was quiet again, Amy said, "Okay, now, guys, will someone tell me exactly what's missing?"

"A bunch of stuff," began Sara.

"Like my diary key," interrupted Kelly.

"And my watch," Melissa added.

"And Lizzy's necklace and mirror, and some money," said Mandy, completing the list of stolen items. "But it's kind of weird 'cause the thief only took coins. All the dollar bills are still in the box."

"That is weird," Amy agreed. She picked up her instant-picture camera, which she had brought to help in the investigation, and took it out of its case. "How did the thief get in?"

"That's just it," replied Mandy. "Of course, the ladder is the only way up here—and we lock that to the tree with a bike lock when we're not here. We lock the trap door, too. I have the key for the ladder, and Kelly has the key for the trap door. The locks are right over there."

Amy went over to the table and picked up the padlock and the bike lock and examined them.

"Doesn't look like anyone tampered with them," said Amy. "Just the same, I better take some pictures of all the evidence there is."

She attached a flashbulb and snapped a picture. As she waited for the picture to appear, she looked around.

"Hey, wait a minute. There's another way someone could have gotten in here."

"How?" demanded Mandy.

"Yeah," said Kelly. "Tell us!"

"Look," said Amy, pointing out the window of the tree house. "That's how."

All the girls rushed to the window and crowded together. Through the thick, sprawling branches they could see that one branch led right to the sill of Lizzy's bedroom window.

"You mean Lizzy did it?" gasped Mandy.

"I bet she did," said Kelly. "I bet she climbed right out of her bedroom window, along that branch, and right in here."

"Yeah, but some of *her* things were stolen, too," said Sara.

"Well, so what!" continued Kelly. "She probably took some of her own things just to throw us off the trail."

Amy was upset. "Hey, you guys, wait a minute. We don't know who did it yet. You can't just go around accusing people without any proof. Don't worry. If I can't solve it, I'll get my friend, Hawkeye, over here to help."

"Hawkeye!" shrieked Sara. "He's a *boy*!"

"Yeah," said Mandy. "And if the boys from the hideout really did it, I bet Hawkeye would be on their side."

Amy rolled her green eyes. "Oh, all right. But I'm going to take some more pictures, and if I have any trouble figuring this out, I'm still going to show 'em to Hawkeye."

The members of the Girls-Only Tree-house Club grumbled some more, but finally let Amy do her work. She studied the trap door, leaned through it, and snapped a photo of the thick, old oak tree.

Next, Amy studied the treasure box that had held the things that had been stolen. She took a picture of that, too. Finally, she turned to the window that looked over toward Lizzy's room.

Amy pointed her camera at the tangle of branches and Lizzy's bedroom window, and snapped a final picture.

"Hey, I wonder—"

Amy pointed her camera at the tangle of branches and Lizzy's bedroom window and snapped a final picture. She waited for it to develop, and then studied it. There was something there that wasn't quite right.

Puzzled, Amy sat down to think. Then she remembered something that had happened during the meeting.

"Case closed!" said Amy, turning back to the girls and holding the photograph out for them to see. "I know who the thief was!"

WHO STOLE THE TREASURES FROM THE TREEHOUSE?

S O L U T I O N
See page 85

The Case of Lucy's Loss

"What do you mean, they can't find my ski*th*?" cried Lucy. She made a face and stuck her tongue out in the space where her two front teeth were missing.

Amy hung up the phone and turned to her sister, a puzzled look on her face.

"Sorry, Luce, but the guy at the news-paper said *all* the prizes are missing. It's weird. He said the skis were definitely loaded onto the train that arrived this morning, but they're missing now."

"Oh, no! What *th*tupid luck!" howled Lucy. "I want my ski*th* now! We got all that *th*now last night and here I am without any ski*th*!"

Amy rolled her green eyes. "Listen, Lucy, screaming isn't going to help any." She thought a minute, then picked up the phone.

"Who are you calling?" asked Lucy, rubbing her nose.

Amy said into the phone, "Hawkeye?"

Lucy leaped up and grabbed the receiver from Amy. "My ski*th* are gone!"

"Lucy!" said Amy, yanking the phone back.

Pouting, Lucy slumped down in a chair, swinging her legs.

"Hawkeye, remember how Lucy won a pair of cross-country skis in that Christmas contest the newspaper sponsored? Well, all of the skis have disappeared!"

Amy listened and nodded. "Yeah." She twisted the phone cord in her hand.

"Well," she continued, "the guy at the newspaper office said the skis should've arrived at the train station this morning. But he says the railroad car is empty. Not a single pair of skis. It really stinks, huh?"

"You bet!" muttered Lucy.

Amy listened, then glanced at her watch. Lucy leaned forward, trying to hear what Hawkeye was saying.

"Sure," said Amy, fiddling with a red pigtail. "See you in a minute."

Amy hung up the phone and headed for the coat hooks in the kitchen. Lucy was half a step behind her.

"Maybe it wa*th* a real train robbery!" said Lucy excitedly.

"Maybe," Amy replied. "Hawkeye and I are going to check things out at the train station. You can come with us, but only if you promise—and I mean really promise—not to get in the way."

Lucy started shoving her feet into her blue moon boots and crossed her heart. "I do, I do, I do," she said solemnly.

In a few minutes, Hawkeye, Amy, and Lucy were trudging through the deep snow to the Lakewood Hills train station. Although the heavy snowfall had ended that morning, not all of the streets had been plowed yet.

They found the new station master, Mr. Legrand, shoveling snow off the loading dock.

"We came down to find out about the missing skis," said Hawkeye.

"Now what the heck do you think you're going to find?" grumbled Mr. Legrand. "I told that guy at the newspaper everything I know. And now he sends a bunch of kids to snoop around!"

"I ju*tht* want my ski*th*!" said Lucy loudly.

"Cut it out, Luce!" said Amy.

"Yeah, but—"

Amy turned to her sister and raised a warning finger. "Lucy, you promised!" Turning to Mr. Legrand, she said, "Sorry, but she's real upset."

"She won one of the pairs of skis," Hawkeye explained.

"Yeah, yeah," said Mr. Legrand, shoveling again. "Well, all I know is the freight car finally arrived this morning. There was a bill of lading stapled to the door—fifty pairs of skis. That's what it said."

He tossed the shovel aside and led the way over to a huge freight car nearby. Hawkeye and Amy peered inside. It was completely empty. Lucy hopped up and down, trying to look.

"Could I please see the bill of—what is it called?" asked Hawkeye.

"Yeah, what'*th* that?" said Lucy.

"It's a list of everything that was loaded onto the freight car," Amy told her.

"Help yourself," said Mr. Legrand gruffly.

He pointed to a sheet of paper that was stapled to the door and mumbled something under his breath as he went back to shoveling. Hawkeye and Amy read it carefully.

"It looks pretty official," said Amy.

"Yeah, but—" Hawkeye frowned. He examined the bill of lading again, then scanned the railroad cars and tracks. He felt there was something wrong here, but he couldn't put his finger on it.

Hawkeye pulled off his mitten. In a second, he had fished his sketch pad and pencil out of his jeans pocket.

Lucy hung her head. Near tears, she mumbled, "I'm never gonna get my ski*th*."

Lucy trudged through the snow over to a bench. She brushed the snow off it and sat down, looking miserable. Hawkeye started sketching the train car and other details of the station. Mr. Legrand stopped shoveling to watch over Hawkeye's shoulder. Amy went over to her sister.

"Come on, Luce, cheer up," she said. "You'll get your skis."

"Never! I'm never going to get 'em!" the younger girl moaned.

A couple of minutes later, Hawkeye finished his drawing and called out.

"Hey, Amy," he said, holding up his drawing. "Come here and take a look at this!"

Amy hurried over and looked at the sketch. "Hawkeye, you're right!"

Lucy yelled, "What i*th* it? What did you guy*th* find?"

"What do you mean, they can't find my skith?" cried Lucy.

"Shh," whispered Hawkeye. "Don't say anything, Lucy, but I think I know what happened to your skis. Let's call Sergeant Treadwell!"

WHAT HAD HAPPENED TO LUCY'S SKIS?

See page 87

The Secret of the Band-Room Bandit

"See you later, Mom!" said Hawkeye, grabbing his blue windbreaker.

"Hawkeye, you didn't finish your breakfast!" Mrs. Collins called as Hawkeye darted out the kitchen door into the garage.

"This is an emergency, Mom," Hawkeye yelled over his shoulder. He opened the garage door and began wheeling his ten-speed out. "There's been a robbery at school. Amy just called—we've got to get over there fast! See you tonight!"

"But the rain!" she called after him as he swung up on his bike.

As Hawkeye shot down the driveway, his windbreaker instantly soaked in the downpour, he shouted back, "But, Mom! The robbery!"

Seconds later, he rode up Amy's driveway and pounded on the garage door. There was a click, and the next moment the large door began to roll upward.

"That was fast," Amy greeted him, zipping up her bright green rain slicker. "Man, you're soaked."

Hawkeye looked down at himself and grinned. "I guess it's raining harder than I thought. Come on, let's go!"

They climbed on their bikes and barreled down the driveway.

"So what else do you know about the robbery?" asked Hawkeye, lifting his feet as he rode through a puddle.

Amy peeked out from beneath the hood of her slicker. "Well, Mr. Chekov called me just before I called you. All the band uniforms were sent out last week to be cleaned. They were due back today. But when Mr. Chekov got to school—no uniforms. He called the delivery man, and he said that he'd brought the band uniforms over early this morning. But they're gone now."

"Oh, boy, what a bummer—the big band concert for Memorial Day is tomorrow,"

Hawkeye said as they rounded the corner and headed across the school parking lot.

Amy nodded. "Mr. Chekov sounded really upset. Without the uniforms, the band will probably have to back out of the concert."

"What a raw deal," said Hawkeye, frowning. "Especially since this is Mr. Chekov's first big concert here."

Mr. Chekov was the new music teacher at Lakewood Hills Elementary, and Hawkeye and Amy had grown to like him a lot. At the beginning of the year, with his heavy accent and bulky clothes, he had seemed strange to most of the kids. But his hearty laugh and friendliness had soon made him one of the school's most popular teachers.

As Amy hopped off her bike and locked it up, she said, "Hawkeye, your hair looks like over-boiled macaroni!"

Hawkeye snapped his lock shut and leaped over a big puddle.

"Yeah? Well, you—" In mid-sentence, his foot slipped and landed in the middle of the mess. "Yuk!" he shouted, pulling his muddy running shoe out of the puddle. Disgustedly, he muttered, "Aw, forget it!"

The two sleuths hurried inside, out of the rain.

"Is terrible, no?" asked Mr. Chekov in his thick Russian accent. "But I am so glad you come to Mr. Chekov. You *v*ill help me, yes?"

"Sure," said Hawkeye, grinning as he tried to comb some of the rain out of his blond hair.

"Is good." Mr. Chekov clapped his hands. "Now, I *v*ill tell you *v*hat happened. I, Mr. Chekov, comes to school this mornin*k* to prepare for b*ee*g, b*ee*g dress rehearsal. I come in and no uniforms. One b*ee*g zero. None. No. Nothin*k*. You got me?"

Amy smiled. "We got you, Mr. Chekov. So then what did you do?"

"I call to Presto Cleaners and I talk to delivery man. He says he *v*as here at seven this mornin*k* and he hung all uniforms in band room."

"And when you got here, they were gone?" asked Hawkeye.

"Double zero. Nothin*k*." Mr. Chekov shrugged. "The delivery man said all uniforms *v*ere covered by plastic. He said, too, that one very, very nice student help him. They make many trips. He tell me he put uniforms on rack in that corner," the music teacher added, pointing to the back of the room.

"Did he get the kid's name?" asked Amy.

"No." Mr. Chekov shook his head. "All thirty-five uniforms gone. This is b*ee*g loss." He spread his arms wide.

"I wonder who'd want to stop the band from playing," said Hawkeye.

48

"Hey." Amy turned to Mr. Chekov. "Didn't you have some trouble with that trumpet player last week? Frank—Frank—"

"Frank Barney." Mr. Chekov scratched his bushy brown hair. "A little trouble, yes, but Frank is good boy."

"Some of the kids have been saying that Greenhill Elementary School's band wanted to play but wasn't invited," said Hawkeye. "I heard it was because their band was so rowdy last year. Maybe they stole the uniforms, hoping they'd be invited at the last minute."

"Maybe, maybe." Mr. Chekov sighed. "Is terrible, no?"

"Is terrible, yes," agreed Amy. "Do you mind if we look around?"

Mr. Chekov stepped aside. "Please to look!"

Hawkeye scanned the room carefully and took his sketch pad out of the back pocket of his jeans. Leaning against the wall, he began sketching the room.

Amy unzipped her rain slicker and glanced around the room. Out in the hall, students, drenched from the rain, had started hurrying in.

"Can you think of anyone else who might have had a grudge against the band?" she asked Mr. Chekov.

His dark eyes wide with concern, Mr. Chekov replied, "Vell, the janitor, Mr. Haley,

Hawkeye said, "It just doesn't seem possible that thirty-five band uniforms would disappear. Something's fishy."

is sometimes angry vith me. You see, the band must to practice many hours and that makes beeg mess for him." He swept an arm around to indicate the large room.

"Is he here now?" Amy asked.

"Is sick," replied Mr. Chekov. "He is sick today."

Hawkeye was almost finished with his sketch. Mr. Chekov came over and watched him add the finishing touches.

"You have remarkable gift, Hawkeye," he said.

"Thanks, Mr. Chekov. It's fun," Hawkeye replied.

Looking at his completed drawing, Hawkeye said, "It just doesn't seem possible that thirty-five band uniforms would just disappear like that. Something's fishy."

Amy peered over his shoulder, studying the sketch. Suddenly she snapped her fingers.

"Check this out," she said, pointing to two things in the picture.

"Way to go, Amy!" exclaimed Hawkeye.

Amy turned to the band instructor. "Mr. Chekov, I think we've found some evidence. And I have a hunch about who the culprit is!"

WHO STOLE THE BAND UNIFORMS?

See page 89

The Case of the Famous Chocolate Chip Cookies

"Wow!" exclaimed Hawkeye. He was sitting next to Amy in the back seat of Sergeant Treadwell's police car. Sarge had called Hawkeye and Amy and asked them to come along with him to see if they could help solve another case.

"You mean," Hawkeye said, "someone broke into Grandma Johnson's Cookie Works and stole a recipe—and that's *all*?"

The sergeant steered the car toward the edge of town. "Well, it was a very valuable secret recipe. It was the one for her famous chocolate chip cookies."

"Oh, yum!" exclaimed Amy. "Those are the best cookies in the entire world! And they're even made right here in Lakewood Hills."

"Maybe not for much longer," Sergeant Treadwell commented. "If someone else starts making that cookie, it could put Grandma Johnson right out of business."

"That'd be terrible," said Hawkeye, sketch pad and pencil in hand.

They arrived at the cookie factory a few minutes later and hurried inside. The rich, tempting smell of baking cookies greeted them. Grandma Johnson was pacing up and down in front of a row of huge copper kettles.

With her white hair and round, pink face, Grandma Johnson looked like Mrs. Santa Claus. But her appearance was misleading. She was also one of the most successful businesswomen in Lakewood Hills.

"Oh, Sergeant Treadwell, I'm so glad you're here," said Grandma Johnson, shaking his hand and sounding relieved. "And Hawkeye and Amy, thanks so much for agreeing to help. This theft could be a very big threat to the Cookie Works. If someone else uses my secret recipe, this place could go down the drain."

"Do you know how the thieves got in?" asked Sergeant Treadwell, his eyes wandering over a rack of cookies.

"You bet," Grandma Johnson replied, adjusting her apron. "Through the back door by my office. They practically ripped it right off its hinges. Broke the lock and everything."

"Do you have any idea who might want to steal your secret recipe?" asked Amy.

"Goodness, Amy. All sorts of people." Grandma Johnson paused and grinned. "Competition is pretty hot. It's dog eat dog, as we say in the cookie biz."

"Where did you keep the recipe?" Hawkeye asked.

The white-haired woman looked pained and pointed toward her office at the rear of the building. "In a cookie jar on my desk, naturally. That jar has been with me ever since I moved the business from my kitchen to this plant. It's sort of a symbol of the homemade touch that's my trademark. All my employees knew I kept the secret recipe in it."

Sergeant Treadwell frowned. "How about anyone else?"

Grandma Johnson pushed her glasses up on her nose. "Well, Gertrude Olsen knew about the cookie jar, for one. She runs the bake shop in Stillwater. She came in here just last week wanting to buy that very recipe. I gave her a flat no. She got quite huffy and stormed out."

Hawkeye's eyes darted around the huge baking room filled with mixing tables, refrigerators, and large ovens. Except for a fine layer of flour covering much of the equipment, the baking room was very clean.

"Everything seems pretty much in order," Sergeant Treadwell observed. He closed his eyes as he caught a whiff of melting chocolate. Then he snapped out of his daydream. "Um, could you show us where they broke in?"

The store owner nodded and led them to the rear of the building. She leaned toward them as they passed a man in a tall white hat who was mixing brown sugar and butter.

"That's Ned," she whispered. "Sort of a loner, always brooding, but a good worker."

Hawkeye's eyes grew wide. "Wow, look at all that butter and sugar! That's going to make a ton of dough!"

Grandma Johnson smiled. "Oh, it will, indeed."

The white-haired woman nodded toward a man who was pulling a tray of over a hundred cookies from the oven.

"That's Frank," she said. "He's been with me for many years. Always worried about money."

Sarge licked his lips hungrily as they walked past a five-foot-long rack filled with brownies cooling.

"Are these people your only employees?" asked Amy, trying to keep her mind on the case.

"Well, there's John, our supply man, but he's been home with a broken ankle all week. He said he'll be back as soon as his doctor says he can use crutches. And there's Bertha, who's in charge of packaging," Grandma added. "She works in the back room. That's all of us."

They followed Grandma Johnson past the last copper kettle, where giant beaters were mixing a few dozen eggs. Near the back door was her office.

Grandma took a plate of cookies from her desk and said, "Please help yourselves." Then she shook her head. "I just kept the recipe in the jar for fun. I always knew I should have kept it in a safe. Guess I'm just too trusting."

Sarge's face lit up as he reached for a polite handful of the cookies. "A safe would probably have been a good idea," he agreed.

Hawkeye took a bite of a cookie and walked over to the door.

"Were these footprints here when you came in this morning?" he asked, noticing some tracks of flour dust.

"Why, yes," Grandma Johnson replied. "Of course, some of these are my tracks. I was so alarmed when I discovered the broken lock that I came right in and rushed to my desk. That's when I discovered that my secret recipe had been stolen!"

Amy checked out the cookie jar. "Maybe there are some fingerprints here."

"Yeah, maybe, but—" Hawkeye said, still looking around. "Something tells me

"Were those footprints here when you came in this morning?"
Hawkeye asked Grandma Johnson.

there's some other clue here, right in front of us."

He pulled out his sketch pad and pencil and began to draw. Quite sure of himself, he moved his pencil rapidly over the paper. The answer, he knew, was somewhere in what he saw. And drawing the scene with all its details would help him solve the mystery.

Hawkeye was just putting the finishing touches on the sketch when it struck him.

"Of course!" said Hawkeye, a big smile spreading across his face. "I know who stole your secret recipe, Grandma!"

WHO STOLE GRANDMA JOHNSON'S SECRET COOKIE RECIPE?

SOLUTION
See page 91

THE CASE OF THE VANISHING PRINCE

THE CATWALK CHASE PART 2

What Happened in Volume 5

In the first part of this story, Mrs. von Buttermore had taken Hawkeye and Amy to the Florida amusement park, FunWorld. While there, Hawkeye and Amy made friends with Umberto, who was desperately trying to escape two big, sinister men who were following him.

In an effort to shake off the men, Hawkeye, Amy, and Umberto all jumped onto the Haunted Kingdom ride. But during the ride, Umberto was kidnapped and Hawkeye and Amy learned that he was really the crown prince of Madagala.

Hawkeye and Amy went back to the Haunted Kingdom ride's chamber of doors, which was the last place they had seen Umberto. Just as Hawkeye discovered which door the kidnappers had used when they escaped with Umberto, the two big men who had been following Umberto arrived on the scene.

Hawkeye said, "Umberto has been kidnapped—and I know which way they went!"

The Catwalk Chase

Deep inside the Haunted Kingdom, Hawkeye and Amy stood stock still as the two men Prince Umberto was trying to escape from stared down at them. Screams from people in other parts of the ride echoed all around them.

One of the men had Amy by the shoulder. She tried to move away. "Gulp. I think we're in for it, Hawkeye," she said, her voice shaking.

Hawkeye glanced at his sketch. "Yeah, but—"

The big man with the moustache stepped forward and, in a gravelly voice, demanded, "What are you kids doing?"

"Um, we're looking for our friend," said Hawkeye.

"Yeah, we kind of lost him," Amy added weakly.

"Lost him?" shouted the stocky man. "You lost Umberto?"

"Oh, no," said the first man. "Umberto—gone! Not again. What will the king say?"

Amy scratched her head. "Wait a minute. Who are you guys, anyway?"

"You mean," said Hawkeye, "*you* don't have Umberto?"

"We should, but we don't," said the man with the moustache. "We're his bodyguards. I'm Mario and he's Geno."

"It's a very difficult job," said Geno. "Prince Umberto is always trying to lose us. It's sort of a game for him, I'm afraid."

Examining his drawing, Hawkeye said, "Well, I'm afraid this time it isn't a game. Something terrible has happened to him. I think he's been kidnapped!"

"What!" the two men exclaimed.

Hawkeye and Amy told them about the cut seat belt, the last time they had heard Umberto scream, and the bloody newspaper they had found.

"Oh, no!" cried Mario. "Whoever did it must want the crown jewels of Madagala as ransom! They're priceless—not only in their value alone, but also because of the number of tourists they bring to our country each year."

"We must save the prince!" said Geno loudly. "But where did they go? How did they get out of here? I came from that way," he added, pointing to one end of the chamber.

The other guard pointed in the opposite direction. "And I came in the other way. Obviously all these doors are just painted on the wall—so where could the prince be?"

Hawkeye held up his drawing. "Look, there are all sorts of painted doors over there, but one of them is real—the one where there's a shadow under the doorknob."

"You're right," said Amy. "It's the only way they could have gotten out of this chamber without being seen by at least one of us. What are we waiting for? They must have taken Umberto through that door!"

Just as one of the train of cars roared into the area, the four of them ducked out the door. The riders' screams of fright surrounded them.

The door opened onto a narrow metal walkway—a catwalk—that crossed high over a dark area the size of a gym. The space below was filled with huge pieces of heavy, churning machinery, the inner workings of the Haunted Kingdom. From far across this space came a cry.

"Help!"

Amy pointed to a couple of dark figures who were struggling with a smaller figure.

"It's Umberto!" she shouted.

"Yeah," said Hawkeye, straining to see the figures across the gloomy room. "And it looks like they're carrying him away!"

"Stop!" shouted Mario, trying to squeeze past Hawkeye on the narrow walkway. "Release the boy!"

"Keep on fighting, Umberto!" yelled Hawkeye.

One of the dark figures turned. "You can tell your king that he won't get his son back until he gives us the crown jewels!"

Carrying Umberto, the two figures turned and made their way along the twisting catwalks.

Amy, the fastest of the bunch, began running after the kidnappers. Hawkeye was next, followed by the two bodyguards.

The high, narrow catwalks, suspended some twenty or thirty feet above the grinding machinery, swayed and shook. Like tiny bridges, the walkways split and crossed each other, one branch going off one way, another leading another way. Their shoes made an enormous racket as they banged on the metal walkway. In the distance they heard yet another train of cars roaring through the Haunted Kingdom.

The kidnappers, carrying Umberto, disappeared up one catwalk and around a corner. Hawkeye leaned against one of the railings, trying to see where they had gone.

"I can't see them," he said, stretching far over the railing.

Suddenly the railing loosened and fell away. Hawkeye lost his balance and tumbled off the catwalk.

"Help!" he cried as he fell through the air.

Amy turned. "Hawkeye!"

The bodyguards lunged forward but were too late to grab him. They reached the spot where Hawkeye had fallen just as the broken railing clattered on the heavy machinery far below.

Amy grabbed onto a post and leaned over the edge of the catwalk. Afraid of what she might see, she half-closed her green eyes.

"Haw . . . Hawk . . . Hawkeye—" she gasped.

Nothing. Nothing but emptiness. Finally, a moment later, they heard a frightened voice.

"H-h-help!" Hawkeye's voice could barely be heard above the din of the machinery. "Someone—help! I can't hang on much longer!"

Amy and the bodyguards leaned farther over the edge of the catwalk. Below them, Hawkeye was desperately hanging by one hand from a pipe below the catwalk.

"Hawkeye!" shouted Amy. "If you let go, I'm never going to speak to you again!"

Hawkeye glanced down at the sharp, pointed metal machinery below him.

"You can say that again." His voice quavered as he struggled to hang on. "Hurry— I'm slipping!"

Mario lay down on his stomach. He stretched his long arm toward Hawkeye as far as he could.

"I can't reach him!"

"You've got to!" shouted Amy. She dropped to her knees and grabbed the body-guard by his ankles. "Lean farther, I'll balance you!"

Geno also grabbed Mario by his ankles. Mario inched forward, straining to reach Hawkeye.

"I—I—" Hawkeye called through clenched teeth as he hung in the darkness. "I can't hold on. I'm—I'm slipping!"

"Hawkeye!" screamed Amy.

Just as Hawkeye's hand began to slip, Mario grabbed him by the wrist. Groaning, he struggled to pull the boy up. As he slid backward, the guard inched Hawkeye upward. Then Geno leaned over the edge of the catwalk and took Hawkeye by the other hand.

"One, two, three!" grunted the two guards.

Almost like magic, they yanked Hawkeye back up onto the catwalk. As white as a ghost, Hawkeye moved away from the edge and shook his head in shock.

He turned to Amy. "Whew." He took a deep breath. "We should get a couple of these guys for the soccer team."

Amy rolled her eyes. "Oh, brother. That was *too* close. Are you all right?"

Hawkeye nodded and took another breath. "Thanks," he said, smiling weakly at the bodyguards.

The bodyguards stood up and brushed themselves off. Just then they heard a noise up ahead. It sounded as if a series of switches were being flipped. Then they heard a loud hissing noise. Finally, in the distance they heard the squeal of a heavy steel door opening and a clang as it closed.

"Umberto!" shouted Mario. He and Geno squeezed past Hawkeye and Amy and hurried on.

Hawkeye wiped his forehead. "What are we waiting for?"

He and Amy followed, their quick steps banging on the metal catwalk. But just as they caught up with the bodyguards, they were all engulfed in a cloud of fog. The kidnappers had turned the fog machine so that, instead of sending the fog up to the Haunted House, it was pumping it at them.

"I can't see anything!" yelled Hawkeye, feeling his way along. "Amy, where are you?"

"Ouch. That was me. You just stepped on my heel," she complained, hopping while she fixed her running shoe. "We're never going to catch those kidnappers now—they're going to get away with Umberto for sure!"

Abruptly, they heard a loud smash. Hawkeye and Amy froze.

"Did something explode?" asked Hawkeye.

"No, look! The fog's clearing!" said Amy.

Mario had simply smashed and broken the fog machine with his huge fist.

"There's been a slight change in the weather," said Geno, smiling.

All four of them broke into a run again. There was only one catwalk here, and the kidnappers were certain to have gone in this direction.

But then the catwalk split. It branched off into a "T." Each of the two branches ended in a heavy steel door. There were buttons, switches, and levers everywhere, and a huge sign that read "DANGER: HIGH VOLTAGE!"

"Which way did they go?" asked Amy, tugging at her red hair in frustration. "Oh, no. Now we're never going to catch them!"

Geno ran up to one of the doors; Mario ran to the other. But both doors were locked—and couldn't be budged.

Hawkeye said, "There's got to be a clue somewhere here that'll tell us which way they went! Amy, you search for clues—I'll do a sketch."

While Hawkeye did the fastest drawing he had ever done in his life, Amy looked everywhere, searching and hoping to find some clue, some sign that would tell them which way the kidnappers had taken Prince Umberto.

Finally Mario said, "We'll just have to break the doors down!"

"But which one first?" asked Hawkeye. "If we're wrong, they'll have gotten away by the time we break down the second one."

"This one," said Geno.

"No, this one!" Mario insisted, tugging frantically at his moustache.

"Hold on!" shouted Hawkeye. "Let me look at my sketch for a minute before you do anything! There's just got to be some clue here that'll tell us which way they went."

Hawkeye and Amy held the sketch between them, studying each detail intently. Suddenly Amy broke the tense silence.

Hawkeye said, "There's got to be a clue somewhere here that'll tell us which way they went!"

"Look! Umberto left us a clue—I know which door the kidnappers took!"

WHICH DOOR HAD THE KIDNAPPERS CHOSEN?

See page 93

SOLUTIONS

The Case of the Grand Canyon Rescue

Lucy figured out that the sixth line in the note said, "I'm in the shade." Then Amy realized that if the girl was in the shade in the morning, the "w" in the letter was the beginning of the word "west." That told them where the girl was.

Before it got ripped, the note had read:

Help
I hurt my leg this morning
when I fell off my burro
and I can't move.
Please hurry, because I'm
very thirsty, even though
I'm in the shade.
I'm on the west
side of Elephant Rock.
Jessie.

They rushed back to camp and radioed the news to John, the park ranger. An hour later, he made it over to the west side of Elephant Rock and found the girl, who had broken her ankle. She hadn't been able to climb on the burro, so she had tied the note to her saddle.

The ranger brought the girl back to camp. Just as the sun was setting, the helicopter arrived and flew her to the nearest medical center.

The Mystery of the Lily Switcher

The glass in one of the window-panes didn't match the glass in the rest of the panes. The windowpane on the left-hand side of the greenhouse was plain, while all of the other panes had a frosted pattern.

"Whoever stole the lilies broke in through the window and switched the plants," said Hawkeye. "Then the thief replaced the broken window with new glass. I suppose the person who did it hoped that Mr. Spinati would think his plants had just died."

"And I bet it was Gus," added Amy. "He's working at the glass company now. Not only would he know how to replace a broken window in a hurry, but he'd be small enough to fit in through the window frame."

When the police went to question Gus, they found the prize lilies in Gus's kitchen window. The lilies were returned in time for Mr. Spinati to enter them in the Lily Growers' Garden Show. He won, of course.

Mr. Spinati was so grateful to Hawk-eye and Amy that he gave them each fifty dollars of his prize money.

79

The Secret of the Carnival Cowboy

Lucy noticed that there were long shadows in the picture (look at the shadows of the fence and the horse).

"And if this photo really had been taken at noon, as Lance claimed, there wouldn't be any shadows. Right, Lucy?" said Amy.

"Yup," beamed Lucy.

Hawkeye looked at Lance. "I bet you deliberately set your watch at noon to give yourself an alibi."

Lance admitted that he had been lying. He said that he had been smoking behind the garage and had started the fire accidentally. When he had seen that he couldn't put it out by himself, he had run away. Later, he'd set up his alibi with the photograph.

Sergeant Treadwell gave Lance a stern lecture about lying, and then told him that he would have to clean up the mess at the burned garage. The sergeant then treated Lucy, Amy, and Hawkeye to giant chili dogs, cotton candy, and huge strawberry snow cones.

81

The Case of the Purse Snatcher's Snafu

The purse snatcher was one of the "dummies" modeling sportswear. Mr. McGuigan had said there were two dummies by the fire exit, but Hawkeye's sketch showed three.

"He was standing there so perfectly still that I even sketched him without realizing he wasn't a real dummy," Hawkeye said later. "I should've noticed his golf bag and guessed that Mrs. Ratchet's purse might be inside. I didn't think of that until it was almost too late."

"Well, it wasn't," Sergeant Treadwell said as he hustled the purse snatcher off to be booked. "Good work, guys."

Mrs. Ratchet was really grateful. She smiled at Hawkeye and Amy when they gave her her purse back.

"I think that's the first time I've ever seen her do anything but frown," Amy whispered to Hawkeye. "Maybe she's not such a bad egg, after all!"

The Mystery of the Treehouse Troublemaker

"It's simple," explained Amy. "The branch that goes over to Lizzy's bedroom is too thin to hold up even a small person. But it's big enough to hold up a small animal. A small animal like a raccoon!"

Amy remembered that only shiny things had been stolen—like the coins, but not the dollar bills. So she guessed that Lizzy's pet raccoon, Juliet, had broken out of her cage, climbed across the branch to the treehouse, and stolen the shiny treasures.

"Come on!" shouted Kelly.

The whole club climbed down the ladder and ran over to Lizzy's back door. Lizzy took them up to her bedroom and there, inside Juliet's cage, they found the shiny treasures under some shredded newspaper.

The girls were so relieved that they made Juliet the official mascot of the Girls-Only Treehouse Club.

"After all," said Amy, "Juliet is a girl!"

85

The Case of Lucy's Loss

Hawkeye noticed that the freight car with the bill of lading on its side had snow on its roof, but very little snow beneath it.

"Since we got all that snow overnight, I knew that any freight car that came in this morning would have had snow on the ground and railroad ties underneath it, even if the rails were worn clear of snow," explained Hawkeye to Sergeant Treadwell.

"Yeah," said Amy, "but look. One of the other freight cars does have snow underneath it, except for the rails."

Hawkeye said, "I bet Mr. Legrand just switched the bill of lading from the car that came in this morning to an empty car, and then claimed the skis had been stolen."

Sergeant Treadwell checked the other freight cars with snow under them and discovered the missing skis in one of them. Mr. Legrand was arrested. The next day, the newspaper ran a picture of Hawkeye, Amy, and Lucy, with her new skis, on the front page.

87

SOLUTION

The Secret of the Band-Room Bandit

Amy noticed that the floors of the band room were spotlessly clean.

"With all the rain, the rest of the school floors are a mess," she explained. "If the delivery man had delivered the band uniforms—you know, with all the trips and stuff—there would have been some wet footprints and some puddles in the band room, too. I figure he has to be lying."

Mr. Chekov went over to Presto Cleaners and talked to the delivery man, who admitted he had lied. He had dropped the clean uniforms in the muddy school parking lot that morning. Afraid of losing his job, he had rushed the uniforms to another cleaner, hoping they would be ready before anyone noticed they were missing.

Unfortunately, the uniforms didn't get cleaned in time for the dress rehearsal that morning. But they did arrive in time for the big concert the next day—and Mr. Chekov dedicated the first song to Hawkeye and Amy.

The Case of the Famous Chocolate Chip Cookies

Hawkeye noticed that one of the sets of footprints was not an ordinary pair of prints.

"Look," he said, pointing to his drawing, "here are Grandma's prints—see the shape of her high-heeled shoes? Now look at these. You can see only one footprint here. And look at these extra round dots—I think they're prints made by crutches."

"Hawkeye, you're right!" said Amy. "And there is an employee—John—who knows where the recipe is kept and who also could be using crutches!"

Sergeant Treadwell went directly to John's house and brought him into the police station for questioning. John confessed that he had stolen the cookie recipe so that he could start his own cookie shop. At Grandma Johnson's request, Sarge merely lectured John, who promised never to steal again.

Later, Grandma Johnson was so grateful to Hawkeye, Amy, and Sergeant Treadwell for recovering the stolen recipe that she gave them each a case of her famous chocolate chip cookies.

91

The Catwalk Chase

Amy correctly noticed that one of the buttons by the right-hand door wasn't a button at all, but Umberto's ring. The ring, marked "CPU" for "Crown Prince Umberto," was hanging by a fine chain from a lever.

"Look," Amy said, running up and grabbing the ring. "One of the kidnappers had Umberto over his shoulder. Umberto must have put his ring up there when they carried him through the door."

"Way to go, Amy!" exclaimed Hawkeye.

What happens to Prince Umberto? Are Hawkeye and Amy ever able to rescue their young friend? Be sure to read the rest of this four-part series in Volumes 7 and 8 of the **Can You Solve the Mystery?™ series!**

93